Copyright © text and illustrations Century Hutchinson Ltd 1986

All rights reserved

First published in 1986 by Hutchinson Children's Books Ltd
An imprint of Century Hutchinson Ltd
Brookmount House, 62-65 Chandos Place, Covent Garden, London WC2N 4NW

Century Hutchinson Publishing Group (Australia) Pty Ltd
16-22 Church Street, Hawthorn, Melbourne, Victoria 3122

Century Hutchinson Group (NZ) Ltd
32-34 View Road, PO Box 40-086, Glenfield, Auckland 10

Century Hutchinson Group (SA) Pty Ltd
PO Box 337, Bergvlei 2012, South Africa

Designed by Sarah Harwood
Edited by Sarah Ware

Set in Stymie Light, by The Keystroke Mill
Printed and bound in Italy

British Library Cataloguing in Publication Data
Hunt, Roderick, *1939-*
Hippo learns his name.
I. Title II. Gordon, Mike
823'.914[J] PZ7

ISBN 0 09 167220 1

HIPPO
learns his
name

Written by Rod Hunt
Illustrated by Mike Gordon

Hutchinson
London   Melbourne   Auckland   Johannesburg

There once was a time when the king of the animals was the Lion. But one day the other animals said, 'Why should Lion always be king? It's not fair. Let's have a meeting and choose. After all, most of us could do the job just as well.'

After that the animals met every year to choose a new king. Most years they voted for an animal who was brave or strong like Tiger or Elephant, but last year Mouse was king. Mouse was very, very clever, and that's why the animals chose him.

'I wonder if I'll be king this year?' said
Giraffe. 'I think someone tall would do.'

'I stand a good chance,' said Snake.
'I've been nice to everyone all year.'

'We want a king who's good at jokes,'
said Monkey. 'That's what I'm best at.'

'They won't choose me,' Hippopotamus thought sadly. 'They won't choose an animal who can't say his own name.'

It was true. He could say 'Hippo' but he just couldn't say 'Hippopotamus'. It always came out as 'Hippo-p-p-p-pop!'

'The animals won't vote for you,' snapped Crocodile nastily, as the two of them met on the river bank. 'Imagine a king who can't say his name properly.'

Hippopotamus felt himself blushing with shame. 'Why couldn't I have been called Ant or Worm,' he sniffed. 'It's no fun being a hippo-p-p-p-pop when you can't say it.'

A big tear ran down his cheek, over his nose and splashed on to the ground.

After that Hippo kept away from the rest of the animals. He was afraid they might tease him like Crocodile.

Instead he swam sadly up and down in the river. Even if he was bad at saying his name, he was very, very good at swimming.

'I'm worried about Hippopotamus,' said Monkey to the other animals one day. 'He's hardly spoken to any of us for ages.'

Pig, who was quite a wise little animal, said, 'He's upset because he can't say his name properly.'

'Then we must help him,' cried Elephant.

'But how?' asked Snake.

'We don't know,' said the others.

'We'll ask Mouse,' said Pig. 'After all, Mouse is very clever. And he is king of the animals this year. It's his job to know.'

So they asked Mouse, and he said, 'Get
Hippopotamus to say his name and make
him sneeze at the same time.'

'But how?' asked the animals.

'Must I think of everything?' sighed
Mouse. 'Haven't you heard of pepper?'

Later that day the animals called Hippo over to a part of the bank where a branch hung over the water.

Parrot perched on the branch out of sight. He was ready to sprinkle pepper on Hippopotamus's nose.

'Tell us your name,' shouted all the animals. 'Go on. Tell us!'

'Hippo-p-p,' began Hippopotamus and at that moment Parrot shook the pepper all over his face. 'Hippop-p-p-ah-aah Hippo-tisheroo!'

'He called himself Hippo-tisheroo,' said Pig. 'It's a step in the right direction.'

'Mouse's idea was good, but mine is better,' said Crocodile.

'Oh,' said Elephant, 'and what's that?'

'A short sharp shock!' replied Crocodile.

The animals were not sure what Crocodile meant, but they told Hippo to come on to the bank and they asked him his name.

At that moment, Crocodile sank his sharp teeth into Hippopotamus's bottom.

Hippo yelled 'Hippo-poterouch!'

'Hippo-poterouch is an improvement,' said Ant. 'He needs to use his mouth more. I suggest we make him eat a bar of soap.'

'But nobody eats soap,' said Snake.

'Hippopotamus will, if it's hidden in some fruit cake,' said Ant.

Once again the animals called Hippopotamus to the bank. 'We're sorry about that bite on your bottom,' they said. 'Here's some fruit cake. Eat it and say your name.'

Hippo ate the cake in one munch. He said, 'I'm called Hippo-blub-blub-blub!'

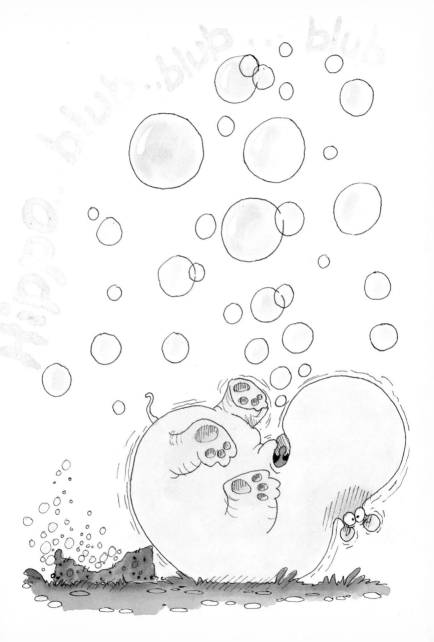

'We've lost ground,' sighed Pig gloomily. 'Hippo-blub-blub-blub is miles off!'

'It's his teeth,' announced Giraffe. 'If we gave him some new ones, I'm sure he would come out with his name.'

'Then let's make him a set,' said Worm.

'Hello Hippopotamus,' said Monkey. 'See what we've got – a new set of gnashers for you. Pop them in and tell us your name.'

Monkey slipped the false teeth into the huge mouth. Hippo spoke with a loud whistle and said 'I'm Hippo-sausages!'

Then a terrible thing happened. The whistle was so loud that all the animals jumped with surprise and Mouse fell into the river. He was swept into the middle where he gave a tiny cry for help, and sank out of sight.

The animals were horrified. They stood and watched helplessly.

'Do something, somebody,' cried Giraffe, who quite hated the water.

'It's no good,' sobbed Elephant, 'He's gone, and we'll never see him again.'

But all the animals had forgotten that Hippo was very good at swimming. He took a big breath and dived down under the green water. Just when he thought his lungs would burst, he saw Mouse being turned over and over by the current.

Very gently, Hippopotamus caught Mouse
in his huge mouth and swam to the surface.
No-one spoke as he laid the limp little
body on the bank.

Mouse just lay there very still with his
tiny eyes closed.

'Shall I kiss him better?' asked Elephant.

Mouse opened his eyes at once and said, 'No thanks! I'm quite all right.'

'Hurray!' roared Lion. 'We should give Mouse a party to celebrate.'

'No,' said Mouse. 'Hippo's the hero. What sort of party would you like, Hippo?'

'A Hippo Party, Mouse,' said Hippo, shyly.

Everyone gasped but Hippo smiled.

'A Hippo-Party-Mouse! Hippo-pot-a-Mouse! Hippo-pot-a-mus!' cried Hippo with glee.

All the animals clapped and cheered. At last, Hippopotamus could say his name!

Can you guess who was made king of the animals that year?